Dear Parents and Educators,

Welcome to Penguin Young Readers! As parents and educators, you know that each child develops at his or her own pace—in terms of speech, critical thinking, and, of course, reading. Penguin Young Readers recognizes this fact. As a result, each Penguin Young Readers book is assigned a traditional easy-to-read level (1–4) as well as a Guided Reading Level (A–P). Both of these systems will help you choose the right book for your child. Please refer to the back of each book for specific leveling information. Penguin Young Readers features esteemed authors and illustrators, stories about favorite characters, fascinating nonfiction, and more!

The Cow in the House

LEVEL 2

GUIDED READING LEVEL **H**

This book is perfect for a **Progressing Reader** who:
- can figure out unknown words by using picture and context clues;
- can recognize beginning, middle, and ending sounds;
- can make and confirm predictions about what will happen in the text; and
- can distinguish between fiction and nonfiction.

Here are some **activities** you can do during and after reading this book:
- Titles: The author chose the title *The Cow in the House* for her book. Why do you think she picked that title? Pretend you are the author of this story. What title would you pick and why?
- Discuss the ending of this story. Why did the man think his house was quiet? Do you think the wise man gave him good advice? Why or why not?
- Make Connections: Have you ever thought your house was too noisy? What did you do about it? What lessons can you learn from this story?

Remember, sharing the love of reading with a child is the best gift you can give!

—Bonnie Bader, EdM
  Penguin Young Readers program

*Penguin Young Readers are leveled by independent reviewers applying the standards developed by Irene Fountas and Gay Su Pinnell in *Matching Books to Readers: Using Leveled Books in Guided Reading*, Heinemann, 1999.

Penguin Young Readers
Published by the Penguin Group
Penguin Group (USA) Inc., 375 Hudson Street, New York, New York 10014, USA
Penguin Group (Canada), 90 Eglinton Avenue East, Suite 700, Toronto, Ontario M4P 2Y3, Canada
(a division of Pearson Penguin Canada Inc.)
Penguin Books Ltd., 80 Strand, London WC2R 0RL, England
Penguin Group Ireland, 25 St. Stephen's Green, Dublin 2, Ireland (a division of Penguin Books Ltd.)
Penguin Group (Australia), 250 Camberwell Road, Camberwell, Victoria 3124, Australia
(a division of Pearson Australia Group Pty. Ltd.)
Penguin Books India Pvt. Ltd., 11 Community Centre, Panchsheel Park, New Delhi—110 017, India
Penguin Group (NZ), 67 Apollo Drive, Rosedale, Auckland 0632, New Zealand
(a division of Pearson New Zealand Ltd.)
Penguin Books (South Africa) (Pty.) Ltd., 24 Sturdee Avenue,
Rosebank, Johannesburg 2196, South Africa

Penguin Books Ltd., Registered Offices: 80 Strand, London WC2R 0RL, England

Text copyright © 1997 by Harriet Ziefert. Illustrations copyright © 1997 by Emily Bolam. All rights
reserved. First published in 1997 by Viking and Puffin Books, imprints of Penguin Group (USA) Inc.
Published in 2012 by Penguin Young Readers, an imprint of Penguin Group (USA) Inc.,
345 Hudson Street, New York, New York 10014. Manufactured in China.

The Library of Congress has cataloged the Viking edition under the following
Control Number: 96040057

ISBN 978-0-14-038349-2   10 9 8 7 6 5 4 3 2 1

PENGUIN YOUNG READERS

LEVEL
PROGRESSING READER
2

The Cow in the House

retold by Harriet Ziefert
illustrated by Emily Bolam

Penguin Young Readers
An Imprint of Penguin Group (USA) Inc.

4

Once upon a time,

a man lived in a

noisy old house.

CREAK!

The bed creaked.

The chair squeaked.

The roof leaked.

"This house is too noisy,"

said the man.

Drip
Drip

Squeak

The man went to town

to see a wise man.

"What should I do?" he asked.

"My house is too noisy.

The bed creaks.

The chair squeaks.

The roof leaks."

"Here's what you should do,"

said the wise man.

"Get a cow.

And keep it in your house."

The man thought it was a silly idea.

But he said, "I'll do it."

The cow said, *Moo, moo!*

The bed creaked.

The chair squeaked.

The roof leaked.

"My house is still too noisy,"

said the man.

"So get a donkey," said the wise man.

"And keep it in your house."

The man thought it was

a very silly idea.

But he said, "I'll do it, anyway."

"Now my house is even noisier,"
said the man.

"So get a sheep,"
said the wise man.
"And keep it in
your house."

The man thought it was a stupid idea.

But he said, "I'll do it, anyway."

The sheep said, *Baa, baa!*

The donkey said, *Hee-haw!*

The cow said, *Moo, moo!*

The bed creaked.

The chair squeaked.

The roof leaked.

"I can't live in my house!"

said the man.

"So get a cat," said the wise man.

"And a dog, too!"

Another dumb idea, thought

the man.

But he did it, anyway.

The dog said, *Woof, woof!*

The cat said, *Meeow, meeow!*

The sheep said, *Baa, baa!*

The donkey said, *Hee-haw!*

The cow said, *Moo, moo!*

The bed creaked.

The chair squeaked.

The roof leaked.

Now the man was mad.

Very mad!

He yelled at the wise man.

"I told you my house was too noisy!

You told me to get animals.

Noisy, noisy animals!

I am going crazy from the noises

they make!"

The wise man waved his arms.

"Do what I tell you!" he shouted.

"Put the dog out of the house!

Put the cat out of the house!

And the sheep!

And the donkey!

And the cow!

Put them all out!"

BAA BAA

So the man put them all outside.

He went back inside

and got into bed.

The bed creaked.

The chair squeaked.

The roof leaked.

Drip

squeak

"Oh, what a quiet house!"

said the man.